TRAVELS THROUGH TIME

TRAVELS THROUGH TIME

EDITED BY

Isaac Asimov
Martin Harry Greenberg
Charles Waugh

ILLUSTRATED BY

Thomas Leonard

RAINTREE PUBLISHERS
MILWAUKEE TORONTO MELBOURNE LONDON

Copyright © 1981, Raintree Publishers Inc.

Library of Congress Number: 81-8521

1 2 3 4 5 6 7 8 9 0 85 84 83 82 81

Printed in the United States of America.

Library of Congress Cataloging in Publication Data

Main entry under title:

Travels through time.

    Contents: Introduction / Isaac Asimov — The
assassin / Robert Silverberg — The innocents'
refuge / Theodore L. Thomas — [etc.]
    1. Science fiction.   2.   Children's stories.
[1.   Space and time — Fiction.   2.   Short stories]
I.   Asimov, Isaac, 1920-   II.   Greenberg,
Martin Harry.   III.   Waugh, Charles.   IV.   Leonard,
Thomas, 1955-   ill.
PZ5.T732   [Fic]   81-8521
ISBN 0-8172-1726-6   AACR2

"The Assassin" © 1957 by Greenleaf Publishing Company.
    Reprinted by permission of the author.
"The Innocents' Refuge" © 1957 by Columbia
    Publications, Inc. Reprinted with permission of the
    author.
"The Good Provider" © 1952 by Marion Gross. By
    permission of Barthold Fles, Literary Agent.
"The Immortal Bard" © 1953 by Palmer Publications,
    Inc. Reprinted by permission of the author.
"The Figure" © 1947 by Street and Smith Publications
    Inc. Reprinted by permission of Lawrence LeShan.

Contents

Introduction

ISAAC ASIMOV

In our history books we read about the past. In American history, we learn about Columbus's voyage and how he discovered America. We learn about the colonists settling Virginia and landing on Plymouth Rock — of the American Revolution and George Washington — of the Civil War and how Abraham Lincoln was assassinated —.

It's a long, fascinating story and many people, I imagine, couldn't help thinking sometimes what fun it might be to live in some of those older times and experience some of the excitement of those days.

If one could live in the past, knowing what would happen, it might be tempting to try to change history. Suppose you knew that John Wilkes Booth was out there somewhere getting ready to try to kill President Lincoln. Maybe you could stop him so that Lincoln could finish his term as president and live out his life. That might change American history after 1865 completely.

It works the other way round, too. The times we live in are pretty exciting, also. We are so used to our own surroundings that we take them for granted, but imagine if someone who lived in George Washington's time could travel two centuries into his future and be alive right now.

Imagine how excited he would be when he saw airplanes and television. Something as simple as a tall building would astonish him and he would wonder how anyone could get to the top. He wouldn't know what an elevator was.

And suppose you found yourself two centuries in your future, when it was nearly 2200 A.D. What would *you* find? It's hard to say. We might not even be able to imagine some of the things that everyone would take for granted then. — Or perhaps civilization would have gone to smash and you would find only ruins.

It's only a hundred years ago since people began to write such "time-travel" stories. In 1899, Mark Twain wrote "A Connecticut Yankee in King Arthur's Court". In that book, an American of the 1880s moved thirteen centuries into the past and found himself with the Knights of the Round Table. Naturally, he tried to introduce some of the modern things he knew about and if you read the book you'll see what happened.

Mark Twain's American, however, had moved into the past by accident. In 1896, H. G. Wells went further. He wrote "The Time Machine" in which, for the first time in literature, a device was imagined that could go into the future or past at will by manipulating controls — just as an automobile can move north, south, east or west.

Since then, time-travel stories have been among the most popular kind of science fiction that has been written. Almost every science fiction writer has tried his hand at it.

Yet there is an important catch. Time-travel by means of a machine that can be controlled like an automobile is probably impossible. It isn't that it just happens to be impossible right now. There is good reason to think it may be forever impossible.

Usually, when science fiction writers know that something is impossible they are careful not to use it in their stories. Time-travel is one of the very few exceptions to this rule. There are so many exciting things that time-travel makes possible that science fiction writers just can't bear to give it up. They continue to write them — impossible or not — and the stories in this book are examples.

The Assassin

ROBERT SILVERBERG

The time was drawing near, Walter Bigelow thought. Just a few more adjustments, and his great ambition would be fulfilled.

He stepped back from the Time Distorter and studied the complex network of wires and tubes with an expert's practiced eye. TWENTY YEARS, he thought. Twenty years of working and scrimping, of pouring money into the machine that stood before him on the workbench. Twenty years, to save Abraham Lincoln's life.

And now he was almost ready.

Bigelow had conceived his grand idea when still young, newly out of college. He had stumbled across a volume of history and had read of Abraham Lincoln and his struggle to save the Union.

Bigelow was a tall, spare, rawboned man standing better than six feet four — and with a shock he discovered that he bore an amazing resemblance to a young portrait of the Great Emancipator. That was when his identification with Lincoln began.

He read every Lincoln biography he could find, steeped himself in log-cabin legends and the texts of the Lincoln-Douglas debates. And, gradually, he became consumed with bitterness because an assassin's hand had struck Lincoln down at the height of his triumph.

"Awful shame, great man like that," he mumbled into his glass one night in a bar.

"What's that?" a sallow man at his left asked. "Someone die?"

"Yes," Bigelow said. "I'm talking about Lincoln. Awful shame."

The other chuckled. "Better get yourself a new newspaper, pal. Lincoln's been dead for a century. Still mourning?"

Bigelow turned, his gaunt face alive with anger. "Yes! Yes — why shouldn't I mourn? A great man like Lincoln —"

"Sure, sure," the other said placatingly. "I'll buy that. He was a great president, chum — but he's been dead for a hundred years. One hundred. You can't bring him back to life, you know."

"Maybe I can," Bigelow said suddenly — and the great idea was born.

It took eight years of physics and math before Bigelow had developed a workable time-travel theory. Seven more years passed before the first working model stood complete.

He tested it by stepping within its field, allowing himself to be cast back ten years. A few well-placed bets, and he had enough cash to continue. Ten years was not enough. Lincoln had been assassinated in 1865 — Friday, April 14, 1865. Bigelow needed a machine that could move at least one hundred twenty years into the past.

It took time. Five more years.

He reached out, adjusted a capacitor, pinched off an unnecessary length of copper wire. It was ready. After twenty years, he was ready at last.

Bigelow took the morning bus to Washington, D.C. The Time Distorter would not affect space, and it was much more efficient to make the journey from Chicago to Washington in 1979 by monobus in a little over an hour, than in 1865 by mulecart or some other such conveyance, possibly taking a day. Now that he was so close to success, he was too impatient to allow any such delay as that.

The Time Distorter was cradled in a small black box on his lap; he spent the hour of the bus ride listening to its gentle humming and ticking, letting the sound soothe him and ease his nervousness.

There was really no need to be nervous, he thought. Even if he failed in his first attempt at blocking Lincoln's assassination, he had an infinity of time to keep trying again.

He could return to his own time and make the jump again, over and over. There were a hundred different ways he could use to prevent Lincoln from entering the fatal theater on the night of April 14. A sudden phone call — no, there were no telephones yet. A message of some kind. He could burn down the theater the morning of the play. He could find John Wilkes Booth and kill him before he could make his fateful speech of defiance and fire the fatal bullet. He could —

Well, it didn't matter. He was going to succeed the first time. Lincoln was a man of sense; he wouldn't willingly go to his death having been warned.

A warm glow of pleasure spread over Bigelow as he dreamed of the consequences of his act. Lincoln alive, going on to complete his second term, President until 1869. The weak, ineffectual Andrew Johnson would remain Vice-President, where he belonged. The south would be rebuilt sanely and welcomed back into the Union; there would be no era of carpetbaggers, no series of governmental scandals and no dreary Reconstruction era.

"Washington!"

Moving almost in a dream, Bigelow left the bus and stepped out into the crowded capitol streets. It was a warm summer day; soon, he thought, it would be a coolish April evening, back in 1865. . . .

He headed for the poor part of town, away from the fine white buildings and gleaming domes. Huddling in a dark alley on the south side, he undid the fastenings of the box that covered the Time Distorter.

He glanced around, saw that no one was near. Then, swiftly, he depressed the lever.

The world swirled around him, vanished.

Then, suddenly, it took shape again.

He was in an open field now; the morning air was cool but pleasant, and in the distance he could see a few of the buildings that made the nation's capitol famous. There was no Lincoln Memorial, of course, and the bright needle of Washington's Monument did not thrust upward into the sky. But the familiar Capitol dome looked much as it always had, and he could make out the White House further away.

Bigelow refastened the cover of the Distorter and tucked the box under his arm. It clicked quietly, reminding him over and over again of the fact that he was in the year 1865 — the morning of the day John Wilkes Booth put a bullet through the brain of Abraham Lincoln.

Time passed slowly for Bigelow. He made his way toward the center of town and spent the day in downtown Washington, hungrily drinking in the gossip. Abe Lincoln's name was on everyone's tongue.

The dread War had ended just five days before with Lee's surrender at Appomattox. Lincoln was in his hour of triumph. It was Friday. The people were still discussing the speech he had made the Tuesday before.

"He said he's going to make an announcement," someone said. "Abe's going to tell the Southerners what kind of program he's going to put into effect for them."

"Wonder what's on his mind?" someone else asked.

"No matter what it is, I'll bet he makes the South like what he says."

He had never delivered that speech, Bigelow thought. And the South had been doomed to a generation of hardship and exploitation by the victorious North that had left unhealing scars.

The day passed. President Lincoln was to attend the Ford Theatre that night, to see a production of a play called "Our American Cousin."

Bigelow knew what the history books said. Lincoln had had an apprehensive dream the night before: he was sailing on a ship of a peculiar build, being borne on it with great speed toward a dark and undefined shore. Like Caesar on the Ides of March, he had been warned — and, like Caesar, he would go unheeding to his death.

But Bigelow would see that that never happened.

History recorded that Lincoln attended the performance, that he seemed to be enjoying the play. And that shortly after ten that evening, a wild-eyed man would enter Lincoln's box, fire once, and leap to the stage, shouting, "Sic semper tyrannis!"

The man would be the crazed actor John Wilkes Booth. He would snag a spur in the drapery as he dropped to the stage, and would break his leg — but nevertheless he would vanish into the wings, make his way through the theater he knew so well, mount a horse waiting at the stage door. Some days later he would be dead.

As for President Lincoln, he would slump forward in his box. The audience would be too stunned to move for a moment — but there was nothing that could be done. Lincoln would die the next morning without recovering consciousness.

"Now he belongs to the ages," Secretary of State Stanton would say.

No! Bigelow thought. It would not happen. It would not happen. . . .

Evening approached. Bigelow, crouching in an alley across the street from the theater, watched the carriages arriving for the performance that night. Feeling oddly out of place in his twentieth-century clothing, he watched the finely-dressed ladies and gentlemen descending from their coaches. Everyone in Washington knew the President would be at the theater that night, and they were determined to look their best.

Bigelow waited. Finally, a handsome carriage appeared, and several others made way for it. He tensed, knowing who was within.

A woman of regal bearing descended first — Mary Todd Lincoln, the President's wife. And then Lincoln appeared.

For some reason, the President paused at the street-corner and looked around. His eyes came to rest on the dark alley where Bigelow crouched invisibly, and Bigelow stared at the face he knew almost as well as his own: the graying beard, the tired, old, wrinkled face, the weary eyes of Abe Lincoln.

Then he rose and began to run.

"Mr. President! Mr. President!"

He realized he must have been an outlandish figure, dashing across the street in his strange costume with the Time Distorter clutched under one arm. He drew close to Lincoln.

"Sir, don't go to the theater tonight! If you do —"

A hand suddenly wrapped itself around his mouth. President Lincoln smiled pityingly and turned away, walking on down the street toward the theater. Other hands seized Bigelow, dragged him away. Blue-clad arms. Union soldiers. The President's bodyguard.

"You don't understand!" Bigelow yelled. He bit at the hand that held him, and got a fierce kick in return. "Let go of me! Let go!"

There were four of them, earnest-looking as they went about their duties. They held Bigelow, pummelled him angrily. One of them reached down for the Distorter.

In terror Bigelow saw that his attempt to save Lincoln had been a complete failure, that he would have to return to his own time and try all over again. He attempted to switch on the Distorter, but before he could open the cover rough hands had pulled it from him.

"Give me that!" He fought frantically, but they held him. One of the men in blue uniforms took the Distorter, looked at it curiously, finally held it up to his ear.

His eyes widened. "It's ticking! It's a bomb!"

"No!" Bigelow shouted, and then watched in utter horror as the soldier, holding the Distorter at arm's length, ran across the street and hurled the supposed bomb as far up the alley as he could possibly throw it.

There was no explosion — only the sound of delicate machinery shattering.

Bigelow watched numbly as the four men seized his arms again.

"Throw a bomb, will you? Come on, fellow — we'll show you what happens to guys who want to assassinate President Lincoln!"

Further down the street, the gaunt figure of Abe Lincoln was just entering the theater. No one gave Bigelow a chance to explain.

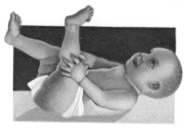

The Innocents' Refuge

THEODORE L. THOMAS

The door slid shut behind him and he leaned against it, his head tilted back, his breath sounding loud in the stillness of the house.

The woman stepped into the hall and saw him against the door. Silently she crossed the hall and flung herself on him. His arms encircled her and he pressed her to his breast.

For a long moment the two stood holding each other. And then side by side but still clinging together they walked into the great room. Gently he placed her on a divan. He cupped her chin in his hand and tipped her head up and looked into her tear-dimmed eyes. His other hand stroked the shimmering waves of golden hair that fell across her shoulders.

"It is all right," he said. "Lyon is in good hands; they will take good care of him."

She tried to smile but could not; instead the tears came again. She struggled to her feet and said, half-crying, "Why must they do this to us? Why must they take my baby away? Have they no heart? Have they no understanding?"

He slipped an arm around her shoulders and said, "Yes, my darling, they have. But our little boy was — well, you know how he was. There is no place for him in our civilization."

"No place." She spat the words. "How do they know? He was only two weeks old; he was a fine, strapping handsome baby boy. How can they be sure he was — he was different."

He dropped his arm from around her and said, "My darling, we have been over this before. They can tell; they do not make mistakes. His brain is just not there. Much of it is missing and can never grow in. No, my dear; there can be no doubt that our child was subnormal."

She raised her head and said, "I don't care. He is my baby, and I would have taken care of him if they had let me. Why do they want to kill him? It wasn't his fault."

He passed his hand across his face. "I know," he said, "and I feel much as you do. But they have reasons. They said that our boy couldn't begin to cope with the problem of modern living. Someone would have to watch him every minute of his life. If you and I were to care for him, we would have time for little else. We would grow embittered, resentful of a society into which our son could not fit. So they say it is better for us to be hurt sharply now than to watch our child grow up."

"I don't care what they say. After forty thousand years of civilization I still think they are beasts. I am glad you have taken Lyon where they cannot get him and murder him."

He slowly took off his robe and tossed it over the divan. He walked to a glass wall and gazed out into the deep night. "You know," he said softly, "I had the strangest feeling tonight when I took Lyon back; I had the feeling that the way was being smoothed for me. It was uncanny."

She sat down on the divan and said, "What do you mean?"

"Well, I am not certain. But everything happened for my benefit. The guards around the Time Machine were unusually lax. Just before I got in, Lyon began to cry. You know how loud his cry is, but the guards fifty feet away didn't even seem to hear it. Furthermore, the machine had already been warmed up; all I had to do was give the dial a random spin and hit the switch. And coming back was the same thing. The guards never happened to look where I was hiding when I came out of the building. It shouldn't be that easy; those Time Machines are the best guarded things in the country."

She looked at him quietly for a moment. "Well, what do you think it means?"

"I don't know," he said. He stared out into the night and then continued. "Now that I've been through it, everything is beginning to make sense." He turned to face her. "Look. A subnormal child — let's face it, an idiot — is born once in about ten million births. The policy states that they should be put to sleep. But have we ever heard of that happening?"

She stiffened at the word *idiot*, but she said simply, "No."

"On the other hand, everyone has heard how the parents of those children take them back in time in the Machine, and leave the child among the primitives. Yet no one has ever heard of any citizens being able to use the Machine for any other purpose. Now doesn't that seem strange?"

Slowly she nodded. "Yes. It does. Do you — do you think — is it on purpose?"

"I don't know." He began pacing about the spacious room. "Look. No one knows except us, and the doctors, that our child was not normal. We certainly will never tell anyone what we have done, except our close friends. It must be the same with other parents. Well then, why is it that this particular use of the Time Machine is so widely known? There are so few subnormal children that you would think no one would know of it. And when you balance that with the fact that an ordinary fellow like me can walk into the most closely-guarded Machine on Earth, use it, and walk out again — darling, you *must* be right. They let me do it so that they would not have to put Lyon to sleep. They are on our side after all." And he swiftly crossed to her side and swept her up in his arms.

She held him tightly, then suddenly pushed him away. "But why? Why torment us this way? Why make us think they want to

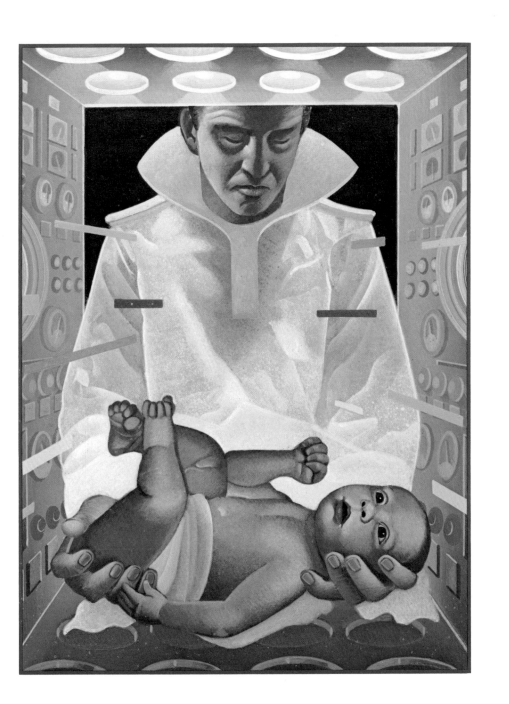

kill our baby? All they need do is tell everybody that subnormal children will be sent back in time to the primitives. Why must they cause such anguish?"

He dropped his arms and stepped away and pulled reflectively at his lower lip. He said, "That is right; there seems no need — wait." He stepped up to her and grasped her shoulders and looked into her eyes. "Tell me. If Lyon were not faced with death, would you agree to sending him back to the primitives? Think, now; would you?"

Her head fell and she stared at the floor. Finally she shook her head. "No," she said, "No. It is too uncertain. The primitives are idiots themselves — savages, too. I know too little about them for me to agree to send my child back among them. No, I would never agree unless my child were faced with death."

He dropped his hands and smiled at her. "That is the answer, my darling. By pretending to want to destroy our subnormal children, they made it possible for us to achieve the courage to send our child back to the ancient peoples."

Wearily he sat down and leaned back and closed his eyes. She sat alongside him and gently pulled his head to her shoulder. "I feel much better," she said softly. "Even though our Lyon must grow up among savages, it can't be so bad. They are not so much his mental superiors that they will harm him. He should be able to hold his own in their civilization."

"Yes, my darling," he said sleepily. "I'm certain he will. I saw his foster parents during the hour I was there. They seemed to love our little Lyon almost as much as we do. In fact they were so impressed with his fine strong body that they are going to keep his first name. They are going to call him Leonardo — Leonardo da Vinci."

The Good Provider

MARION GROSS

Minnie Leggety turned up the walk of her Elm Street bungalow and saw that she faced another crisis. When Omar sat brooding like that, not smoking, not "studying," but just scrunched down inside of himself, she knew enough after forty years to realize that she was facing a crisis. As though it weren't enough just trying to get along on Omar's pension these days, without having to baby him through another one of his periods of discouragement! She forced a gaiety into her voice that she actually didn't feel.

"Why, hello there, Pa, what are you doing out here? Did you have to come up for air?" Minnie eased herself down beside Omar on the stoop and put the paper bag she had been carrying on the sidewalk. Such a little bag, but it had taken most of their week's food budget! Protein, plenty of lean, rare steaks and chops, that's what that nice man on the radio said old folks needed, but as long as he couldn't tell you how to buy it with steak at $1.23 a pound, he might just as well save his breath to cool his porridge. And so might she, for all the attention Omar was paying her. He was staring straight ahead as though he didn't even see her. This looked like one of his real bad spells. She took his gnarled hand and patted it.

"What's the matter, Pa? Struck a snag with your gadget?" The "gadget" filled three full walls of the basement and most of the floor space besides, but it was still a "gadget" to Minnie — another one of his ideas that didn't quite work.

Omar had been working on gadgets ever since they were married. When they were younger, she hotly sprang to his defense against her sisters-in-law: "Well, it's better than liquor, and it's cheaper than pinochle; at least I know where he is nights." Now that they were older, and Omar was retired from his job, his tinkering took on a new significance. It was what kept him from going to pieces like a lot of men who were retired and didn't have enough activity to fill their time and their minds.

"What's the matter, Pa?" she asked again.

The old man seemed to notice her for the first time. Sadly he shook his head. "Minnie, I'm a failure. The thing's no good; it ain't practical. After all I promised you, Minnie, and the way you stuck by me and all, it's just not going to work."

Minnie never had thought it would. It just didn't seem possible that a body could go gallivanting back and forth the way Pa had said they would if the gadget worked. She continued to pat the hand she held and told him soothingly, "I'm not sure but it's for the best, Pa. I'd sure have gotten airsick, or timesick, or whatever it was. What're you going to work on now that you're giving up the time machine?" she asked anxiously.

"You don't understand, Min," the old man said. "I'm through. I've failed. I've failed at everything I've ever tried to make. They always *almost* work, and yet there's always something I can't get just right. I never knew enough, Min, never had enough schooling, and now it's too late to get any. I'm just giving up altogether. I'm through!"

This *was* serious. Pa with nothing to tinker at down in the basement, Pa constantly underfoot, Pa with nothing to keep him from just slipping away like old Mr. Mason had, was something she didn't like to think about. "Maybe it isn't as bad as all that," she told him. "All those nice parts you put into your gadget, maybe you could make us a television or something with them. Land, a television, that would be a nice thing to have."

"Oh, I couldn't do that, Min. I wouldn't know how to make a

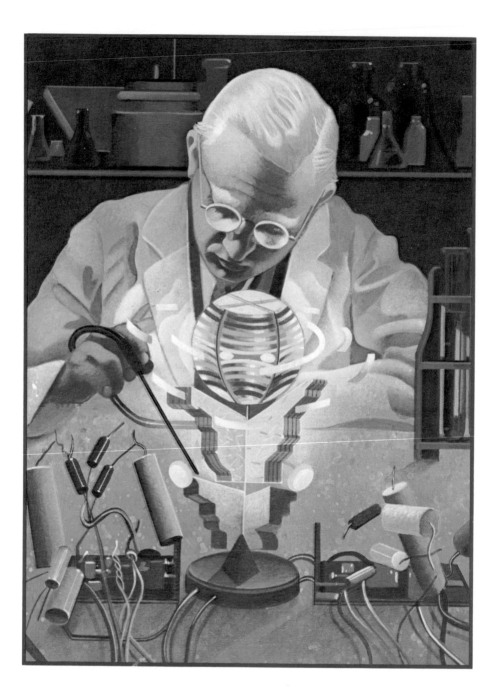

television; besides, I told you, it almost works. It's just that it ain't practical. It ain't the way I pictured it. Come down, I'll show you." He dragged her into the house and down into the basement.

The time machine left so little free floor space, what with the furnace and coal bin and washtubs, that Minnie had to stand on the stairway while Pa explained it to her. It needed explanation. It had more colored lights than a pinball machine, more plugs than the Hillsdale telephone exchange, and more levers than one of those newfangled voting booths.

"Now see," he said, pointing to various parts of the machine, "I rigged this thing up so we could move forward or back in time and space both. I thought we could go off and visit foreign spots, and see great things happening, and have ourselves an interesting old age."

"Well, I don't rightly know if I'd have enjoyed that, Pa," Minnie interrupted. "I doubt I'd know how to get along with all them foreigners, and their strange talk and strange ways and all."

Omar shook his head in annoyance. "The Holy Land. You'd have wanted to see the Holy Land, wouldn't you? You could have sat with the crowd at Galilee and listened to the Lord's words right from His lips. You'd have enjoyed that, wouldn't you?"

"Omar, when you talk like that you make the whole thing sound sacrilegious and against the Lord's ways. Besides, I suppose the Lord would have spoke in Hebrew, and I don't know one word of that and you don't either. I don't know but what I'm glad you couldn't get the thing to work," she said righteously.

"But Min, it does work!" Omar was indignant.

"But you said —"

"I never said it don't work. I said it ain't practical. It don't work good enough, and I don't know enough to make it work better."

Working on the gadget was one thing, but believing that it worked was another. Minnie began to be alarmed. Maybe folks had been right — maybe Omar had gone off his head at last. She looked at him anxiously. He seemed all right and, now that he was worked up at her, the depression seemed to have left him.

"What do you mean it works, but not good enough?" she asked him.

"Well, see here," Omar told her, pointing to an elaborate con-

trol board. "It was like I was telling you before you interrupted with your not getting along with foreigners, and your sacrilegion and all. I set this thing up to move a body in time and space any which way. There's a globe of the world worked in here, and I thought that by turning the globe and setting these time controls to whatever year you had in mind you could go wherever you had a mind to. Well, it don't work like that. I've been trying it out for a whole week and no matter how I set the globe, no matter how I set the time controls, it always comes out the same. It lands me over at Main and Center, right in front of Purdey's meat market."

"What's wrong with that?" Minnie asked. "That might be real convenient."

"You don't understand," Omar told her. "It isn't *now* when I get there, it's twenty years ago! That's the trouble, it don't take me none of the places I want to go, just Main and Center. And it don't take me none of the times I want to go, just twenty years ago, and I saw enough of the depression so I don't want to spend my old age watching people sell apples. Then on top of that, this here timer don't work." He pointed to another dial. "It's supposed to set to how long you want to stay, wherever you want to go, but it don't work at all. Twenty minutes, and then woosh, you're right back here in the basement. Nothing works like I want it to."

Minnie had grown thoughtful as Omar recounted the faults of the machine. Wasn't it a caution the way even a smart man like Pa, a man smart enough to make a time machine, didn't have a practical ounce to his whole hundred and forty-eight pounds? She sat down heavily on the cellar steps and, emptying the contents of her purse on her broad lap, began examining the bills.

"What you looking for, Min?" Omar asked.

Minnie looked at him pityingly. Wasn't it a caution . . .

Purdey the butcher was leaning unhappily against his chopping block. The shop was clean and shining, the floor was strewn with fresh sawdust, and Purdey himself, unmindful of the expense, had for the sake of his morale donned a fresh apron. But for all that, Purdey wished that he was hanging on one of his chromium-plated meat hooks.

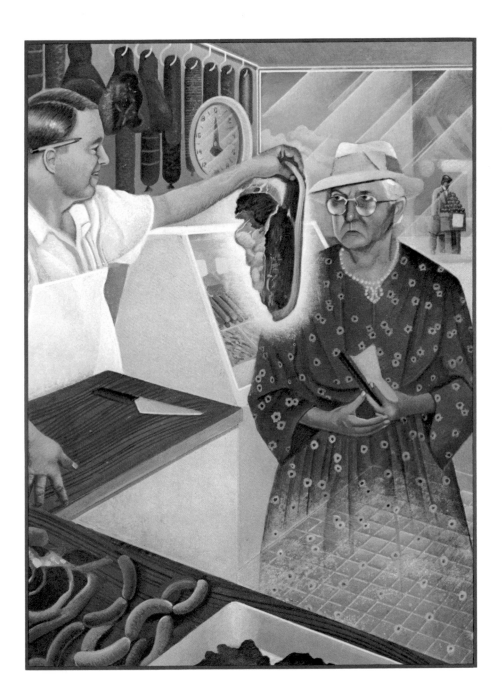

The sky was blue and smogless, something it never was when the shops were operating and employing the valley's five thousand breadwinners. Such potential customers as were abroad had a shabby, threadbare look to them. Over in front of the Bijou old Mr. Ryan was selling apples.

While he watched, a stout, determined-looking woman appeared at the corner of Main and Center. She glanced quickly around, brushing old Mr. Ryan and his apples with her glance, and then came briskly toward Purdey's shop. Purdey straightened up.

"Afternoon, Ma'am, what can I do for you?" He beamed as though the light bill weren't three months overdue.

"I'll have a nice porterhouse," the lady said hesitantly. "How much is porterhouse?"

"Forty-five a pound, best in the house." Purdey held up a beauty, expecting her to change her mind.

"I'll take it," the lady said. "And six lamb chops. I want a rib roast for Sunday, but I can come back for that. No use carrying too much," she explained. "Could you please hurry with that? I haven't very much time."

"New in town?" Purdey asked as he turned to ring up the sale on the cash register.

"Yes, you might say so," the woman said. By the time Purdey turned back to ask her name, she was gone. But Purdey knew she'd be back. She wanted a rib roast for Sunday. "It just goes to show you," Purdey said to himself, surveying the satisfactory tab sticking up from the register, "there still is some money around. Two dollars, and she never even batted an eyelash. It goes to show you!"

The Immortal Bard

ISAAC ASIMOV

"Oh yes," said Dr. Phineas Welch, "I can bring back the spirits of the illustrious dead."

It was the annual Christmas party. Scott Robertson, the school's young English instructor, adjusted his glasses and looked to right and left to see if they were overheard. "Really, Dr. Welch."

"I mean it. And not just the spirits. I bring back the bodies, too."

"I wouldn't have said it were possible," said Robertson primly.

"Why not? A simple matter of temporal transference."

"You mean time travel? But that's quite — uh — unusual."

"Not if you know how."

"Well, how, Dr. Welch?"

"Think I'm going to tell you?" asked the physicist gravely. He looked vaguely about for something to eat and didn't find anything. He said, "I brought quite a few back. Archimedes, Newton, Galileo. Poor fellows."

"Didn't they like it here? I should think they'd have been fascinated by our modern science," said Robertson. He was beginning to enjoy the conversation.

"Oh, they were. They were. Especially Archimedes. I thought

he'd go mad with joy at first after I explained a little of it in some Greek I'd boned up on, but no — no —"

"What was wrong?"

"Just a different culture. They couldn't get used to our way of life. They got terribly lonely and frightened. I had to send them back."

"That's too bad."

"Yes. Great minds, but not flexible minds. Not universal. So I tried Shakespeare."

"*What?*" yelled Robertson. This was getting closer to home.

"Don't yell, my boy," said Welch. "It's bad manners."

"Did you say you brought back Shakespeare?"

"I did. I needed someone with a universal mind; someone who knew people well enough to be able to live with them centuries way from his own time. Shakespeare was the man. I've got his signature. As a memento, you know."

"On you?" asked Robertson, eyes bugging.

"Right here." Welch fumbled in one vest pocket after another. "Ah, here it is."

A little piece of pasteboard was passed to the instructor. On one side it said: "L. Klein & Sons, Wholesale Hardware." On the other side, in straggly script, was written, "Willm Shakesper."

A wild surmise filled Robertson. "What did he look like?"

"Not like his pictures. Bald and an ugly mustache. He spoke in a thick brogue. Of course, I did my best to please him with our times. I told him we thought highly of his plays and still put them on the boards. In fact, I said we thought they were the greatest pieces of literature in the English language, maybe in any language."

"Good. Good," said Robertson breathlessly.

"I said people had written volumes of commentaries on his plays. Naturally he wanted to see one and I got one for him from the library."

"And?"

"Oh, he was fascinated. Of course, he had trouble with the current idioms and references to events since 1600, but I helped out. Poor fellow. I don't think he ever expected such treatment. He kept saying, 'God ha' mercy! What cannot be racked from words in five centuries? One could wring, methinks, a flood from a damp clout!' "

"He wouldn't say that."

"Why not? He wrote his plays as quickly as he could. He said he had to on account of the deadlines. He wrote *Hamlet* in less than six months. The plot was an old one. He just polished it up."

"That's all they do to a telescope mirror. Just polish it up," said the English instructor indignantly.

The physicist disregarded him. He made out a sandwich on the bar some feet away and sidled toward it. "I told the immortal bard that we even gave college courses in Shakespeare."

"*I* give one."

"I know. I enrolled him in your evening extension course. I never saw a man so eager to find out what posterity thought of him as poor Bill was. He worked hard at it."

"You enrolled William Shakespeare in my course?" mumbled Robertson. Even as a fantasy, the thought staggered him. And *was* it a fantasy? He was beginning to recall a bald man with a queer way of talking. . . .

"Not under his real name, of course," said Dr. Welch. "Never mind what he went under. It was a mistake, that's all. A big mistake. Poor fellow." He had the sandwich now and shook his head at it.

"Why was it a mistake? What happened?"

"I had to send him back to 1600," roared Welch indignantly. "How much humiliation do you think a man can stand?"

"What humiliation are you talking about?"

Dr. Welch looked up from the sandwich. "Why, you poor simpleton, you *flunked* him."

The Figure

EDWARD GRENDON

It's a funny sort of a deal and I don't mind admitting that we're scared. Maybe not so much scared as puzzled or shocked. I don't know, but it's a funny deal —. Especially in these days.

The work we have been doing is more secret than anything was during the war. You would never guess that the firm we work for does this kind of research. It's a very respectable outfit, and as I said, no one would ever guess that they maintained this lab, so I guess it's safe to tell you what happened. It looks like too big a thing to keep to ourselves anyhow, although of course it may mean nothing at all. You judge for yourself.

There are three of us who work here. We are all pretty highly trained in our field and get paid pretty well. We have a sign on our door that has nothing whatsoever to do with our work, but keeps most people away. In any case we leave by a private exit and never answer a knock. There's a private wire to the desk of the guy who hired us and he calls once in awhile, but ever since we told him that we were making progress he has more or less left us alone. I promised him — I'm chief here insofar as we have one — that I'd let him know as soon as we had something to report.

It's been a pretty swell setup. Dettner, Lasker, and myself have got along fine. Dettner is young and is an electrical physicist — as good as they make them. Studied at M.I.T., taught at Cal. Tech., did research for the Army, and then came here. My own background is mostly bioelectrics. I worked at designing electroencephalographs for awhile, and during the war I worked at Oak Ridge on nuclear physics. I'm a Jack-of-all-trades in the physics field. Lasker is a mathematician. He specializes in symbolic logic and is the only man I know who can really understand Tarski. He was the one who provided most of the theoretical background for our work. He says that the mathematics of what we are doing is not overly difficult, but we are held back by the language we think in and the unconscious assumptions we make. He has referred me to Korzybski's *Science and Sanity* a number of times, but so far I haven't had a chance to read it. Now I think I will. I *have* to know the meaning of our results. It's too important to let slide. Lasker and Dettner have both gone fishing. They said they would be back, but I'm not sure they will. I can't say I would blame them, but I've got to be more certain of what it means before I walk out of here for good.

We have been here over a year now — ever since they gave me that final lecture on Secrecy at Oak Ridge and let me go home. We have been working on the problem of time travel. When we took the job, they told us that they didn't expect any results for a long time, that we were on our own as far as working hours went, and that our main job was to clarify the problem and make preliminary experiments. Thanks to Lasker, we went ahead a lot faster than either they or we had expected. There was a professional philosopher working here with us at first. He taught philosophy at Columbia and was supposed to be an expert in his field. He quit after two months in a peeve. Couldn't stand it when Lasker would change the logic we were working with every few weeks. He had been pretty pessimistic about the whole thing from the first and couldn't understand how it was possible to apply scientific methods to a problem of this sort.

I still don't understand all the theory behind what we've done. The mathematics are a bit too advanced for me, but Lasker vouches for them.

Some of the problems we had should be fairly obvious. For

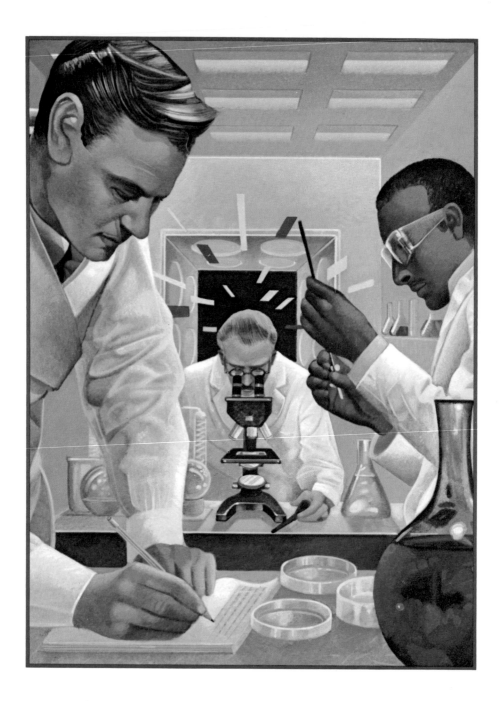

instance, you can't introduce the concept "matter" into space-time mathematics without disrupting the space-time and working with Newtonian space *and* time mathematics. If you handle an "object" — as we sense it as a curvature of space-time — as Einstein does, it's pretty hard to do much with it theoretically. Lasker managed that by using Einstein formulations and manipulating them with several brands of Tarski's non-Aristotelian logic. As I said, we did it, although Dettner and I don't fully understand the mathematics and Lasker doesn't understand the gadget we used to produce the electrical fields.

There had been no hurry at all in our work up to the last month. At the time the Army wrote Dettner and myself and asked us to come back and work for them awhile. Neither of us wanted to refuse under the circumstances so we stalled them for thirty days and just twenty-two days later made our first test. The Army really wanted us badly and in a hurry, and it took a lot of talking to stall them.

What the Army wanted us for was to help find out about the cockroaches. That sounds funny, but it's true. It didn't make the newspapers, but about a year after the New Mexico atom-bomb test, the insect problem at the testing ground suddenly increased a hundred fold. Apparently the radiation did something to them and they came out in force one day against the control station. They finally had to dust the place with DDT to get rid of them.

Looking over the dead insects, all the government entomologists could say was that the radiation seemed to have increased their size about forty per cent and made them breed faster. They never did agree whether it was the intense radiation of the blast or the less intense, but longer continued, radiation from fused sand and quartz on the ground.

New Mexico was nothing to Hiroshima and Nagasaki. After all, there are comparatively few "true bugs" in the desert and a great many in a Japanese city. About a year and a half after Japan got A-bombed, they really swarmed on both cities at the same time. They came out suddenly one night by the millions. It's been estimated that they killed and ate several hundred people before

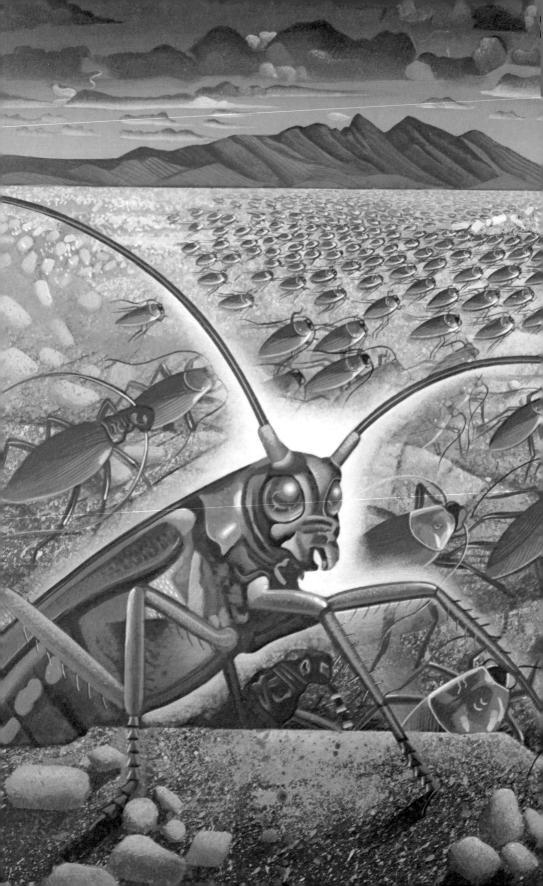

they were brought under control. To stop them, MacArthur had his entire Chemical Warfare Service and a lot of extra units concentrated on the plague spots. They dusted with chemicals and even used some gas. At that, it was four days before the bugs were brought under control.

This time the government experts really went into the problem. They traced the insect tunnels about ten feet down and examined their breeding chambers and what not. According to their reports — all this is still kept strictly hush-hush by the Army, but we've seen all the data — the radiation seems to drive the insects down into the earth. They stay down for awhile and breed and then seem to have a "blind urge" to go to the surface. This urge "seems to affect the entire group made up of an immense number of connected colonies at the same time." That's a quote from their report. One other thing they mentioned is that there were large breeding chambers and some sort of communal life that — to their knowledge — had not been observed in these particular insects before. We told Lasker about it and showed him the reports. He was plenty worried, but he wouldn't say why.

Don't know why I wandered so far afield. I just wanted to explain that if this test wasn't successful, we would probably have to put things off for quite a while. We were interested in the beetle problem as it not only has some interesting implications, but the effect of radiation on protoplasm is a hard nut to crack. However, we had come so far on our time gadget that we wanted to finish it first. Well, we finished and tested it, and now Dettner and Lasker are out fishing. As I said, they probably won't come back.

It was the day before yesterday that we made the final test. Looked at one way, we had made tremendous progress. Looked at another, we had made very little. We had devised an electric field that would operate in the future. There were sixteen outlets forming the sides of a cube about four feet in diameter. When switched on, an electrical field was produced which "existed" at some future time. I know Lasker would say this was incorrect, but it gets the general idea over. He would say that instead of operating in "here-now," it operates in "here-then." He'd get angry every time we'd separate "space" and "time" in our talk and tell us that we weren't living in the eighteenth century.

"Newton was a great man," he'd say, "but he's dead now. If you talk as if it were 1750, you'll *think* and *act* as if it were 1750 and then we won't get anywhere. You use non-Newtonian formulations in your work, use them in everyday speech, too."

How far in the future our gadget would operate we had no way of knowing. Lasker said he would not even attempt to estimate "when" the field was active. When the power was turned off, anything that was in the cube of forces would be brought back to the present space-time. In other words, we had a "grab" that would reach out and drag something back from the future. Don't get the idea we were sending something into the future to bring something back with it, although that's what it amounts to for all practical purposes. We were warping space-time curvature so that anything "here-then" would be something "here-now."

We finished the gadget at three o'clock Tuesday morning. Lasker had been sleeping on the couch while we worked on it. He had checked and rechecked his formulae and said that, if we could produce the fields he'd specified, it would probably work. We tested each output separately and then woke him up. I can't tell you how excited we were as we stood there with everything ready. Finally Dettner said, "Let's get it done," and I pressed the start button.

The needles on our ammeters flashed over and back, the machine went dead as the circuit breakers came open, and there was an object in the cube.

We looked it over from all sides without touching it. Then the implications of it began to hit us. It's funny what men will do at a time like that. Dettner took out his watch, examined it carefully, as if he had never seen it before, and then went over and turned on the electric percolator. Lasker swore quietly in Spanish or Portuguese, I'm not sure which. I sat down and began a letter to my wife. I got as far as writing the date and then tore it up.

What was in the cube — it's still there, none of us have touched it — was a small statue about three feet high. It's some sort of metal that looks like silver. About half the height is pedestal and

half is the statue itself. It's done in great detail and obviously by a skilled artist. The pedestal consists of a globe of the Earth with the continents and islands in relief. So far as I can determine it's pretty accurate, although I think the continents are a slightly different shape on most maps. But I may be wrong. The figure on top is standing up very straight and looking upwards. It's dressed only in a wide belt from which a pouch hangs on one side and a flat square box on the other. It looks intelligent and is obviously representing either aspiration or a religious theme, or maybe both. You can sense the dreams and ideals of the figure and the obvious sympathy and understanding of the artist with them. Lasker says he thinks the statue is an expression of religious feeling. Dettner and I both think it represents aspirations: *per adra ad astra*, or something of the sort. It's a majestic figure and it's easy to respond to it emphatically with a sort of "upward and onward" feeling. There is only one thing wrong. The figure is that of a beetle.

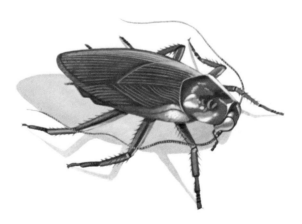